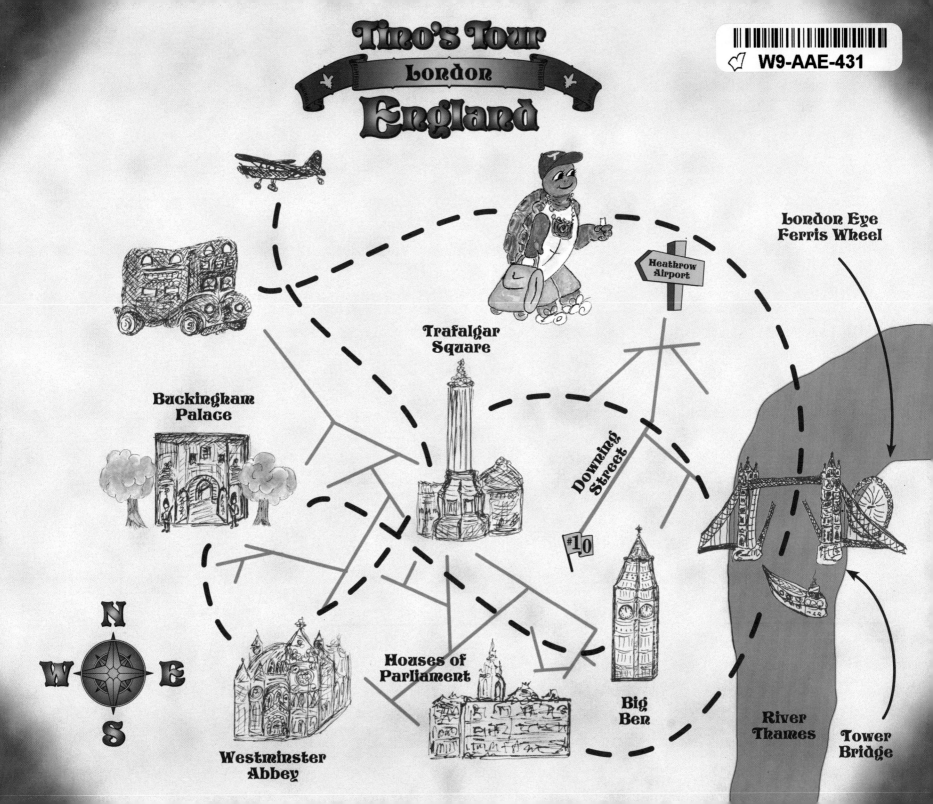

This Book Belongs To:

_____

Tino Turtle Travels
to London, England

by Carolyn L. Ahern
Illustrated by Nealita Burt-Sullivan

To my husband, Don F. Ahern
To the sweet spirit of Dayna Lynn Ahern
— — — — — & — — — — —
To my parents Frank and Sue Bella
Thank you for believing in Tino

Tino Turtle Travels, LLC
8550 West Charleston Boulevard, Suite 102-398
Las Vegas, Nevada 89117
Copyright © 2006-2008 by Carolyn L. Ahern

info@TinoTurtleTravels.com
www.TinoTurtleTravels.com

The artwork was executed in watercolor, watercolor pencils,
graphite and colored inks on Strathmore cold press paper.
The text was set in 14-point New Century Schoolbook,
24-point Barmeno, and 24-point Storybook.

Written and created by Carolyn L. Ahern.

Printed in China.

Revised Edition

Library of Congress Control Number: 2007924998

ISBN-13: 978-0-9816297-0-4

ISBN-10: 0-9816297-0-9

Once upon a time, there was a desert tortoise named Tino. Tino was a happy turtle in his desert habitat, but he had one wish...he dreamed of traveling to see the world.

One night, when in his burrow for his winter sleep, he asks his Fairy God Turtle to make his wish come true.

"Please Fairy God Turtle... let me travel."

As Tino closes his eyes, his Fairy God Turtle waves her magic wand and grants Tino's wish.

Whoosh! Suddenly, Tino is on his way to London, England...far, far away from his desert burrow.

After a long flight in the airplane, Tino arrives at Heathrow Airport. He waves down the first cab he sees.

Tino has met many friends from all over the world by writing letters. He calls these friends his pen pals.

Tino tells the taxi driver, "Please take me to my friend Percy's house. These are the directions, Sir."

When Tino arrives at Percy's Tudor style home, he rings the doorbell and says to himself, "Wow! What a cool house!"

Percy answers the door.

"Hi, I'm Tino Turtle. It is great to meet all of you."

"We are happy to meet you too, Tino," says Percy's dad.

Tino thanks Percy's family for inviting him, and then they all sit down together for supper.

"Mmm, what smells so yummy?" Tino asks.

"Mother has prepared some traditional English favorites for us," Percy replies.

"We're having shepherd's pie and for dessert we'll have bread and butter pudding," says Percy's mother.

"Thank you for this delicious dinner," Tino says.

"Tino, what do you eat for supper back home in the desert?" Percy asks curiously.

"Most of the time, I like to much on grass, plants, and blossoms," Tino replies.

"Tino, let's get a good night's sleep because tomorrow, I plan to take you to my school for show and tell."

"That sounds like fun, Percy. I can't wait!"

Percy shows Tino to his room and they say good night. Tino slips down under the covers and quickly falls asleep.

The next morning, Percy and Tino hurry to the school bus. Suddenly, Percy trips as he is climbing up the school bus steps.

"Jeepers!" he cries out as he grabs Tino's strong shell.

Percy sighs with relief and says, "Oh, thanks, Tino. You saved me from falling and really hurting myself."

Once in the classroom, the teacher, Mrs. Knight, motions Percy and Tino to the front of the class. "Percy, please introduce your new friend to the class," she says.

"This is my friend from America, Tino Turtle. He is my pen pal and the best show and tell we will ever have!" Percy says excitedly.

"Hi, I'm Tino. I am a desert tortoise. A tortoise is a kind of land dwelling turtle. I live in a desert burrow that I dig myself. It keeps me warm during my hibernation."

"Are there any questions you would like to
ask Tino?" Mrs. Knight asks.

"May I touch your shell, please?" asks Diana.

"Sure!" says Tino.

"It's so shiny and hard," Diana says.

"That's to reflect the hot desert sun," says Tino. "It keeps me cool in the summer and warm in the winter. The brown and yellow colors help me hide in the desert sagebrush."

"Is your shell heavy when you walk?" asks Bobbie.

"Sometimes, but I am used to it. When I get tired, I just tuck my head inside and rest," Tino replies.

"Oh, please show us," begs Margaret.

"Ok. Just watch me!" Tino exclaims.

The class looks in amazement when Tino tucks his head inside his shell and pops his head back out again.

The school bell rings, and it's time for a break. Mrs. Knight sends the children outside to play. The students have a great time watching Tino kick up the sand in the schoolyard sandbox.

When the school day is over, the children are sorry to leave their new friend, Tino.

Back on the school bus, Percy asks, "Tino, what was your favorite part of the day?"

"Playing in the sandbox because it reminded me of my desert home in America," Tino replies.

The next day, Percy and Tino begin their London adventure in another bus, a red double-decker.

"Tino, we are going to take a fun boat ride down the River Thames," Percy explains. "This river connects London with the sea. And Tino, be sure to pronounce it *Tems*."

As they exit the bus, they can hear the sound of the boat's horn.

The boat captain calls out: "ALL ABOARD!"

Tino jumps up and down, giggling with excitement. His stubby little legs have never moved so quickly. "Hurry, Percy! Let's get on board!" he says excitedly.

PIER 6

23077

The boat slowly cruises down the river when suddenly the mighty bascules of the Tower Bridge open up to let them pass through.

"TOOT! TOOT!" sounds the horn.

"Look over there, Tino!" Percy says. "That's the London Eye Ferris Wheel. It was built to celebrate the year 2000 millennium."

Tino replies, "Wow! It's amazing!"

"Percy, this is such a blast! I wish I could visit longer."

"Don't worry, Tino. We'll have plenty of time to see the most interesting places."

Suddenly, Tino hears loud bells ringing.

"Listen, Tino!" Percy says. "It's Big Ben striking noon over the Houses of Parliament."

"Who is Big Ben, and what kind of house is that?" Tino asks.

"The Houses of Parliament are part of our government," replies Percy. "That's where our laws are made."

Just then, the boat makes a turn and reveals a tall clock tower, still echoing the twelfth chime.

"And that's Big Ben!" Percy exclaims. "It's one of the biggest clocks in the world!"

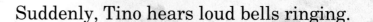

The boat ride ends near London's famous
Downing Street. Percy explains that the
house at Number 10 Downing Street is where
England's Prime Minister lives.
After a long walk through the city, they find
their way to another sight.

"Look over there!" Percy exclaims. "It's Buckingham Palace, our Royal Family's London residence. Quick, Tino, take a picture! We are just in time for the Changing of the Guard."

As they continue their walking adventure, Tino is doing his best to keep up, but he's dragging behind. He has a frown on his face and Percy wonders why.

"Do you want a drink of water, Tino?" Percy asks.

"No thanks, Percy," replies Tino. "I can go a very long time without water."

Percy realizes that Tino's short legs can't keep up. No wonder his little friend is frowning.

Percy looks around for a way to help. He sees
an abandoned wagon lying along the roadside.

He pulls the wagon over to Tino and says,
"Hop in, Pal!"

"Thank you, Percy!" replies Tino.

The wagon rumbles its way down an old cobblestone street.

Suddenly, Tino calls out, "Stop, Percy! This building looks old and scary. Is it haunted?"

"Oh no, Tino...Westminster Abbey is a beautiful church. Kings and queens have been crowned there," Percy explains. "Come on, let's go inside!"

After passing through gigantic wooden doors, they look at the vaulted ceilings in wonder.

Back in the wagon, Tino enjoys the sight of Trafalgar Square.

"The column in the center is called Nelson's column. It honors Admiral Lord Nelson, a leader of England's Royal Navy," Percy says. "Can you see his statue on the top?"

"Yes, I can," Tino replies. "I also see your British flag flying proud and tall. The colors in your flag are the same as ours...red, white and blue."

"Tino, you have learned so much about our city. Now, I'd like to show you the shops in the square," says Percy.

Inside one store, Tino sees a nice watch. He buys it for Percy and says, "Thank you for showing me around your city."

Tino gives the watch to Percy and glances at the time. "Oops! Percy, it's late! I've got to get to the airport!" he says. "I've been having such a good time, I forgot that spring is almost here...my hibernation will soon be over...and my dream will end."

"Oh gosh, Tino, really? I wish you didn't have to go," Percy says.

"Don't worry, Percy. We're pen pals. I'll write to you."

Percy thanks Tino for the watch, and they hug goodbye.

Tino's Fairy God Turtle waves her magic wand, and...

Whoosh! Suddenly, Tino is back home in his desert burrow. His eyes open to the warmth of a spring breeze, the sound of birds singing, and the smell of cactus blossoms.

Tino joyfully says out loud, "Thank you, Fairy God Turtle...'til next time we travel...."

Tino Turtle Travels

Words and Music by Sue Bella